Dear Parent:
Your child's love of reading starts here!

Every child learns to read in a different way and at his or her own speed. Some go back and forth between reading levels and read favorite books again and again. Others read through each level in order. You can help your young reader improve and become more confident by encouraging his or her own interests and abilities. From books your child reads with you to the first books he or she reads alone, there are I Can Read Books for every stage of reading:

SHARED READING
Basic language, word repetition, and whimsical illustrations, ideal for sharing with your emergent reader

BEGINNING READING
Short sentences, familiar words, and simple concepts for children eager to read on their own

READING WITH HELP
Engaging stories, longer sentences, and language play for developing readers

READING ALONE
Complex plots, challenging vocabulary, and high-interest topics for the independent reader

ADVANCED READING
Short paragraphs, chapters, and exciting themes for the perfect bridge to chapter books

I Can Read Books have introduced children to the joy of reading since 1957. Featuring award-winning authors and illustrators and a fabulous cast of beloved characters, I Can Read Books set the standard for beginning readers.

A lifetime of discovery begins with the magical words "I Can Read!"

Visit www.icanread.com for information
on enriching your child's reading experience.

I Can Read Book® is a trademark of HarperCollins Publishers.

Library of Congress Cataloging-in-Publication Data is available.
ISBN 978-0-06-185387-6 (trade bdg.) — ISBN 978-0-06-185386-9 (pbk.)

10 11 12 13 LP/WOR 10 9 8 7 6 5 4 3 2   ❖   First Edition

STRIKE THREE,
Marley!

BASED ON THE BESTSELLING
BOOKS BY JOHN GROGAN

COVER ART BY RICHARD COWDREY

TEXT BY SUSAN HILL

INTERIOR ILLUSTRATIONS BY
ELLEN BEIER

HARPER
An Imprint of HarperCollins*Publishers*

It was spring, and Cassie was going
to her first baseball game.
"Come on, Marley,"
said Daddy.
"You can come, too!"

Cassie and Daddy went
to the baseball field.
They found a place to sit,
and then Daddy told Cassie
the rules.
"The pitcher throws the ball,"
Daddy said.
"The batter swings the bat.
If he misses the ball,
it is called a strike.
Three strikes means he's out."

Daddy looked hard at Marley.

"Your rules are simple,"

he told him.

"Sit. Stay. Got it?"

"Ruff!" Marley barked.

8

Cassie laughed.

"If Marley messes up,

We'll call a strike on him!"

The game began.

The pitcher threw the ball.

It went way over the batter's head.

11

Marley tugged at his leash.

"Sit, Marley," said Daddy.

"That was a wild pitch,"

said Daddy.

"The pitcher must be nervous."

The next pitch went low.

It landed at the batter's feet.

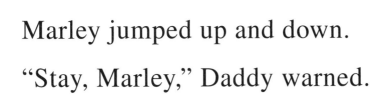

Marley jumped up and down.

"Stay, Marley," Daddy warned.

The pitcher threw the ball again.

This time, the batter hit it

way out over the field.

"They're playing Fetch.

That's my favorite game.

I want to play, too," thought Marley.

Suddenly, Marley broke free

and ran onto the field.

"Sit, Marley! Stay!" yelled Daddy.

16

Marley did not sit.

He did not stay.

Marley kept his eyes on the ball

and ran as fast as he could.

Marley knocked over

the second baseman,

but he didn't stop.

The outfielder dove at Marley
but still Marley didn't stop.

He didn't stop
until he caught that ball!

Then Marley began
to dig like crazy.
The pitcher laughed.
"Sometimes I want
to bury the ball, too," he said.

Daddy and Cassie

chased Marley.

Marley ran away from them.

"Strike one, Marley!" Daddy yelled.

Marley ran to the batter's box
and grabbed the bat in his teeth.
Marley tugged.
The batter tugged back.

Marley tugged harder,

and the batter fell down.

"Strike two, Marley," said Daddy.

Then Marley ran to home base
and grabbed it in his teeth.
"He's stealing home!"
yelled the catcher.

The umpire was mad.

"Uh-oh," said Cassie.

"Strike three, Marley!"

"You're out of the game!"

the umpire yelled.

Marley dropped the base

and stuck out his paw

to shake hands with the umpire.

Daddy grabbed Marley's leash.
By now, everyone was laughing,
even the umpire.
"Sorry," Daddy said to the umpire.
"I guess Marley's not cut out for
the major leagues."

Daddy and Cassie sat down again.

"What did I tell you, Marley?"

said Daddy.

"Sit. Stay.

Is that too much to ask of a dog?"

"Marley didn't sit or stay,"

said Cassie.

"But he did fetch

and shake hands."

Daddy smiled.

"I guess you're right," he said.

"He's a pretty good player,

for a dog."

When the game ended,
the pitcher gave Cassie the ball.
"Thanks to your dog,
I relaxed and pitched my
best game ever!" he said.

Daddy and Cassie hugged Marley.

"We're glad you're on our team,

Marley," said Cassie.